Rutherford
the Unicorn Sheep
Walks the
Dog

By Ariele Sieling

To Joe & Becky—
for all the love you give
to your pets, this one's
for you! :)

2016

This book is dedicated to:

Cricket, Spam, Alex, and Missy

You were the best dog.

Today was a big day! Rutherford was dog sitting two golden retrievers—Cam and Tyler. This was his first time, so he was a little bit nervous.

They seemed friendly though.

"Hi, Cam," Rutherford said. "Do you want to go for a walk?"

Tyler came rushing in from the other room, wagging his tail.
Rutherford laughed. "You must have heard me say walk!"
Tyler wagged his tail harder.

He jumped up on the counter, excited.
"Let's go find your leash, Tyler," Rutherford said.

"Are you ready to go?" Rutherford asked. They headed outside.
Ty wagged his tail even harder. Rutherford thought Ty had a really cute smile.

Cam came out next. Since they were just walking around the yard, Cam didn't need a leash. "Good boy!" Rutherford said, smiling.

It was a beautiful day for walk, and Tyler loved exploring the yard.
There were plenty of interesting things to smell.

All of a sudden, Tyler quit walking and just sat down.
"What's wrong, boy?" Rutherford asked. "Did you run out of things to smell already?
What about that pile of leaves over there?"

Ty just sat there. He wasn't interested in the leaves.
Then Rutherford noticed something lying in the grass.
"Look!" he said. "It's a ball."

That got Tyler's attention! He spun around to look at the ball.

All at once, Tyler took off, pulling on the leash.
"Slow down, Tyler!" Rutherford said. "Wait for me!"

But Tyler was too quick! Rutherford lost his grip on the leash.
"Come back!" Rutherford yelled as Tyler ran across the lawn.

Tyler was having too much fun to go back. He liked the ball.
Rutherford tried chasing him, but his legs were too short to go very fast.

Rutherford decided he needed help.

"Cam?" he said. "Will you please help me catch your brother?"

Rutherford climbed up onto Cam. Cam could go much faster than Rutherford could.

But even Cam was too fast for Rutherford! He lost his grip and rolled
down Cam's long back!

Tyler rushed past in a flurry of fur and excitement. He was kicking the ball with one paw and then chasing it down the grass.

The next thing Rutherford knew he was falling to the ground as Cam chased after Tyler! Cam was having fun too!

Out of the corner of his eye Rutherford could see Tyler making a
mad dash towards the fence.

But when he got back on his feet, he saw that Cam had caught up
with Tyler and the ball. They were playing together.

Rutherford breathed a sigh of relief as Cam brought Tyler back over. "I never should have mentioned the B-A-L-L," Rutherford said carefully.

The two dogs and Rutherford lay down in the grass, enjoying
the spring smells and the warm sun.

"Thank you so much for helping me!" Rutherford exclaimed. He jumped up to give Cam a belly rub, which Cam enjoyed a great deal.

"You must be thirsty from chasing that ball!" Rutherford told Tyler.
"Do you want some water?"

They got up and headed towards the house with Tyler in the lead.

Inside, Rutherford filled the water bowl. It was big enough for him to go swimming in!

After getting a drink, Tyler jumped on the couch.
Rutherford shook his head and laughed—Tyler never stopped moving!

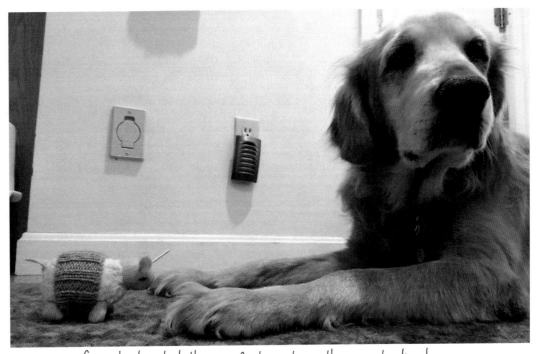

Cam had picked the comfiest spot on the rug to lie down.
Rutherford joined him.

"Thanks for all of your help today," Rutherford said.
Cam sniffed a little and wiggled his eyebrows.

Tyler heard them talking and leaped off the couch to join the conversation.

"You are very fun to play with!" Rutherford told him.
Tyler just grinned.

As both dogs were settled comfortably on the rug, Rutherford smiled.
Dog sitting was a lot of fun!

He couldn't wait to come back the next day!

Did you know that not all animals have homes?

Cam and Tyler are very special dogs. Do you know why? Because they were adopted! But not all animals have a place that they get to call home. Many animals live in places called animal shelters, where they are taken care of by veterinarians and other kind people. But even though they have food and a place to stay, they don't have a family! A shelter is not a home.

Some of them live there because their family had to move and couldn't take them along. Some of them live there because they are sick or injured. Others live there because no one wanted them. Shelter animals have their basic needs taken care of, but what they really want is a home.

What does it take to adopt a dog?

Maybe you've thought about adopting a dog! That's great! But before you adopt, it is important to make sure you are able to take care of the dog, so it never has to go back to the shelter.

If you adopt a pet, make sure you give it food and water *every day*. You also have to make sure they have enough room. If you live in a very small house, it is probably better to get a small dog or another type of small animal for a pet.

Dogs need exercise! This means going for walks, visiting the park, or playing in the yard. Other pets need exercise to—for example, rabbits like to run around and cats like to climb cat trees. Dogs also need to be trained. This can be a lot of fun!

Pets also need to go to the vet sometimes. They have to get shots so they don't get sick, and get check-ups to make sure they are healthy and strong.

Finally, a pet needs a lot of love! They like attention, petting, and lots of time spent with their owner. Maybe one day, you can adopt your very own pet!

Acknowledgements

This book would not be possible without Scott and Bari, the wonderful owners of Cam and Tyler. They were patient, friendly, and willing to let Cam and Tyler play with me in the yard as we photgraphed. Thanks!

I also couldn't have done it without Josh, who helped by playing with the dogs, keeping Rutherford safe, and generally doing whatever needed to be done!

As always, Zoe Cannon does the best covers, and I couldn't do this without her!

About the Author

Ariele Sieling loves animals of all sorts, with dogs ranking quite high on the list. She grew up surrounded by adopted dogs, cats, rabbits, peacocks and a variety of other animals. She is looking forward to the day when she can get a dog. In the meantime, she lives in NH with three cats, and is the author of the *Rutherford the Unicorn Sheep* series, in addition to the YA science fiction series, *The Sagittan Chronicles*.

Cam the Man is a twelve-year-old golden retriever adopted from Tennessee. He has a mellow and laid back personality, and *loves* to get his belly scratched. You can learn more about him by following his Facebook page: Cam the Man!

Ty the Guy is a three-year-old golden retriever from Tennessee. He is a happy-go-lucky, friendly, and energetic dog that loves to play and run. You can learn more about him by following his Facebook page: Ty the Guy!

57014325R00026

Made in the USA
Charleston, SC
05 June 2016